GUILTY OF NOTHING

Kevin King

Copyright 2023 by Kevin King

All rights reserved. This book or any portion thereof may not be reproduced or used in any manner whatsoever without the express written permission of the publisher except for the use of brief quotation in a book review.

Inquiries and Book Orders should be addressed to:

Great Writers Media
Email: info@greatwritersmedia.com
Phone: 877-600-5469

ISBN: 978-1-959493-95-2 (sc)
ISBN: 978-1-959493-96-9 (ebk)

Rev 2/2/2023

For the cure of all mental illness

CONTENTS

1 - Begin 1

2 - Horse Tracks 3

3 - Deaths 5

4 - Arrested 7

5 - Opening 11

6 - Defense 38

7 - Closing 44

8 - Verdict 46

9 - Prison 48

10 - Appeal 53

11 - Media 55

12 - Murders 57

13 - Release 60

14 - Killer 62

15 - End 64

I

BEGIN

Bill Eck was born in Chatham, Illinois, the son of Joe and Marsha Eck. Chatham is a small city a few miles away from Springfield, the capital of Illinois. He grew up in Chatham and went to grade school and high school there. He graduated from Chatham Glenwood High School.

Bill was the star pitcher for the Chatham Glenwood baseball team. He was named the "Central State Eight Player of the Year." Glenwood High School belongs to the Central State Eight Conference.

He received a scholarship from Western Illinois University to play baseball there. He signed his scholarship at the high school. He left for Macomb, Illinois, the following day. He did very well as a college player until he hurt his arm.

But Bill had his college education to fall back on. He was studying to be a civil engineer at Western Illinois University. While at college, Bill met Mary Lewis in his sophomore year. They were married in

Macomb after they both graduated from Western Illinois University. Then Bill and Mary Eck moved to Chicago from Macomb. Bill was hired as a civil engineer for Roy Simon Engineers.

They had two sons and one daughter. The boys were named "Bob" and "Charlie" and their daughter was named Carrie. Charlie played third base for his high school team. Bob was a pitcher for his high school team.

The baseball scouts were looking at the Eck brothers for a possible Major League career. Both of the Eck brothers were excited about the possibility of being a Major League player. Carrie, their sister, was in school in Chicago to be a civil engineer just like her father.

Eddie Eck is the brother of Bill Eck and ran a gas station in Springfield. Eddie wasn't interested in sports but could build a car practically from nothing. Eddie placed Bill's pictures of his high school career on the wall of his gas station. Eddie was very proud of his brother.

Dave and Karrie Mayo were next-door neighbors to the Eck family. Dave Mayo only saw the Eeks on weekends. His days were filled with doing the books for the Roy Simon Engineers. Karrie Mayo worked as the president of the Chicago Park District and tried to make the parks look the best they could be. This kept her busy. Dave and Karrie Mayo had a boy and a girl.

Ed Michaels, another civil engineer at Roy Simon Engineers, was a good friend with Bill. He and Bill hung out together after work and sometimes on the weekends. Roy Simon owned and operated Roy Simon Engineers. He started this business from nothing. Jill Simon, his wife, was the secretary at Roy Simon Engineers. She helped Roy in some of the decision-making of his business.

Father Franks was the pastor where Bill and his family went to church. Bill believed Father Franks always gave a sermon to live by. He taught the Christian life by telling others how Jesus Christ would treat them and how you could treat others the same way.

2

HORSE TRACKS

On weekends, Bill Eck would go to Arlington, Illinois to the horse racing track.

One day, Roy Simon asked Bill, "Bill, I see you a lot at the horse racing track. I own a racehorse. Would you like to see my racehorse?"

Bill answered, "Yes."

Bill and Roy Simon went to the Arlington Horse Racing Track on Saturday, where he also met Steve Gentry and Larry Snyder. Steve Gentry was the horse trainer for "Cupcake", Roy Simon's racehorse. He took care of Cupcake and that kept Steve very busy.

Larry Synder was the jockey for Cupcake. Larry had placed in almost all races with Cupcake.

When at the track, he met Wally and Bill Lester. They were brothers and loved to bet on racehorses, but seemed to not get along with each other.

A week later, Bill was at the racetrack and won at all of the races which he bet on. This was a great day for Bill. He usually was good at winning at most of the races.

Wally Lester came over to him and said, "Bill Eck, I'm going to get you for this. I don't like to lose a race, especially to you."

Bill Lester replied, "Bill Eck, don't worry about it. Wally is just having a hard day today."

Bill Eck didn't know what to think and said, "I don't know what's bothering you but I want nothing to do with you."

He then left the racetrack with his winnings.

Wally Lester said, "I'm going to get this son of a bitch someday."

Bill Lester replied, "Let it go."

Wally and Bill Lester left the racetrack and left Bill Eck alone.

3
DEATHS

Arlington is the home of the Arlington Horse Race Track. It's the home of the Arlington Million, a very famous horse race. It's also a suburb of Chicago.

Debbie Lewis, who was at the horse track a lot, was found dead at the racetrack. She was shot in the head and stabbed fifteen times. Parts of her hair were cut off too. She was found in a garbage dumpster and the police had no clues to this murder.

A week later at a construction site, Maureen Gray and Michele Cook were found in a garbage dumpster. They were killed the same way. Still, the police had no clues on these murders.

Three days later at an apartment complex, Alice Lang and Lorrie Franklin were found in a garbage dumpster. They were killed just like the other three victims were.

Fear was gripping the city. The police still had no clues who this serial killer was. Women were frightened to be alone. Television warned women to be with two or three other people if at all possible.

4

ARRESTED

On one Saturday at the racetrack, Steve Gentry called up Bill Eck and said, "Bill, you're wanted at the stables today for a meeting with Roy Simon."

Bill Eck answered, "Okay." The phone conversation ended.

Bill went to the stables and waited for Roy Simon. Suddenly, Bill was hit by a shovel and knocked out cold.'

A call was placed to 9-1-1. The 9-1-1 operator answered the call and replied, "9-1-1, what's your emergency?"

A person answered, "This is a concerned citizen of the community. The Arlington Horse Track Serial Killer is at the horse racetrack with a bag, looking for his next victim."

The 9-1-1 operator replied, "There's a reward for this person's capture. Can I get your name and address?"

The person responded, "No. I just want to see justice done to this serial killer."

Then the phone clicked and that was the end of the phone conversation.

The Arlington police arrived on the scene and found Bill Eck with a bag. Inside the bag were women's hair, a gun, and a knife. Blood was on the knife and one bullet was still in the chamber of the gun.

Bill was taken to the hospital for his injured head and placed under arrest.

Dale and Tom, brothers and detectives for the Arlington Police Department, worked together on the case.

In the questioning room, Dale Jones asked, "Why did you kill these women?"

Bill Eck asked, "Do what?"

Tom Jones answered, "Don't play innocent with us. You're the serial killer at the racetrack and the other murders."

Bill said, "I didn't kill any of those women."

Tom asked, "Where did the bag come from?"

"I have never before seen this bag in my life."

Dale asked, "Do you expect us to believe this?"

Bill answered, "It's the truth."

Tom said, "Tell this to your attorney. This is an open-and-shut case for us."

Bill was taken back to his jail cell.

An hour later, Bill called Mary up and said, "I need your help. I have been arrested and I'm in jail."

Mary asked, "What are the charges?"

Bill answered, "They're charging me with five counts of murder in the first degree."

Mary asked, "Where are you?"

Bill answered, "In the Cook County jail in Chicago."

Mary replied, "I'll be right over there as soon as possible."

Hours later, Mary met her husband at the Cook County jail.

Bill said, "I was called to a meeting at the horse track stables. I went there alone. Then, something hit me on the back of my head.

I don't remember anything until the police arrived. The Arlington police don't want to listen to my side of the story, but just charge me with five counts of murder in the first degree."

Mary replied, "I'll go to Springfield and see your brother, Eddie. We'll get our attorney, Del Fields, on this case. We'll get you out of here very soon. I love you."

"I love you too."

Mary left the Cook County jail and went home. She told the family where Bill was. They all wanted to do whatever they could to get Bill out of jail.

In Springfield, Mary said to Eddie, "Bill is in trouble."

Eddie asked, "What kind of trouble?"

Mary answered, "Bill is being charged with five counts of murder in the first degree. He never did these crimes."

Eddie said, "I'll place my gas station on the line for Bill who has always been there for me. My gas station means nothing to me if I can't get Bill out of jail."

Mary replied, "That sounds wonderful." Mary left and went to her motel room.

The top story on the news that night was the capture of the Arlington Serial Killer. The media was painting the picture that Bill Eck was guilty as charged before the trial had even begun.

Both Eddie and Mary Eck went to see Del Fields.

Del Fields was the family attorney. He had been the family attorney for a long time. Del handled almost everything from criminal law to business law. The family used him mostly for small legal matters. They had nothing criminal for him to work on until now.

Del asked, "How can I help you two out today?"

Mary answered, "Bill has been arrested for being the Arlington Serial Killer and five counts of murder in the first degree."

Eddie replied, "I'll place my gas station on the line to pay your legal fees. I just want Bill out of jail."

Del responded, "I'll see Bill in Chicago and get him out of jail."

Eddie and Mary left Del's office. Eddie went back to his gas station and Mary went back to her house in Chicago. Del Fields left his office and went to Chicago.

Roy Simon Engineers fired Bill Eck for misconduct after hearing of the arrest.

At the Cook County jail, Del went to see Bill.

Bill said, "Del, I don't know what to do. I'm in jail for something that I didn't do."

Del Fields took out his notebook pad and replied, "You need to listen to me now. I'll get you out of here."

Bill asked, "What do you want me to do?"

Del Fields answered, "Tell me what you know."

Bill said, "I went to the Arlington Horse Track to bet on the horses. Then I was told by the boss's trainer that the boss wanted to see me. I went to the stables and the place where the meeting was supposed to take place alone. Then something hit me on the back of the head. When I woke up, the police were there and they arrested me on these false charges." Del asked, "Who called the police?"

"I don't know."

"Do you still own your gun collection?"

"Yes. It's at our house in Chicago."

"Do you still know how to shoot a gun?"

"Yes. What does that have to do with anything?"

"All of the victims were killed with a gun."

"What can I do about the media? They keep on asking me all types of questions about this crime and why I did it."

"Bill, I'll answer all of the questions from the media from now on. Don't say a damn word."

Del left the Cook County jail, and Bill had hope that maybe this nightmare would soon be over.

OPENING

Both Andy Barrett, the state's attorney, and Del Fields selected the jury for the court trial. Del felt confident that the right jury was chosen, though it was hard to find a jury who hadn't heard something from the media about this case. Del felt sure that the jury would find Bill Eck in nocent.

Andy felt confident that the jury would find Bill Eck guilty as charged.

The highly anticipated media coverage of the trial was to begin. They had the Cook County Courthouse covered at the front entrance and at the courtroom's front en trance. They were waiting for the trial to begin.

The bailiff said, "All rise. The Honorable Tim Brown is presiding over this case."

Tim Brown had been a judge for fifteen years. He loved his job. He seemed to find most of the defendants in his courtroom guilty as charged. Everybody stood up, and Tim Brown walked into the courtroom and sat down. Then everybody else sat down in the courtroom.

Judge Brown said, "We'll hear about bail. The state will go first."

Andy Barrett replied, "The state feels that the defendant, Bill Eck, will run if given the chance. We must think about the public and its safety. This defendant will prey on women if he's out on bail and given the chance to do so."

Judge Brown said, "Now, we'll hear from the defense."

Del Fields responded, "Bill Eck never committed a crime. He has been a good citizen of this community. He will not be a flight risk. He's a good family man."

Judge Tim Brown ruled, "The court rules against the defense and agrees with the state. We must think of the safety of the people of this county first before releasing the defendant back into society. We'll hear the opening arguments from both the state and defense in a week."

The bailiff said, "All rise."

Everybody got up in the courtroom, and Judge Brown left.

The guards then came into the courtroom and placed handcuffs on Bill Eck. They took him back to the Cook County jail.

✦ ✦ ✦

A week later, the bailiff said, "All rise. The Honorable Tim Brown is presiding."

Judge Brown said, "I'll hear opening arguments now."

Andy Barrett was the district attorney. He loved his job and had been doing it for ten years now. He worked on trying to find all defendants guilty as charged.

Andy got up and said, "Thank you, Your Honor. This is an open-and-shut case. We'll prove that the defendant, Bill Eck, is guilty as charged. He was found with the in criminating evidence with him. All of the serial killings in Arlington have stopped since Bill Eck was arrested."

Andy Barrett sat back down.

Del Fields got up and said, "Thank you. Your Honor. We intend to prove that my client, Bill Eck, is innocent of all charges. He's being framed by the real killer who will start these serial killings again after he or she thinks they can get away with these crimes. We intend to prove that the State of Illinois doesn't have an open-and-shut case. After all, Bill Eck has no criminal record, has been a good citizen of the community, votes, pays taxes to the government, and does other duties of a good citizen of the community."

Del sat back down.

Judge Brown said, "We'll hear the state's case first on Monday."

The bailiff replied, "All rise."

Judge Brown got up and left the courtroom.

The guards came into the courtroom and placed handcuffs on Bill Eck. Then the guards escorted Bill Eck back to the Cook County jail.

Everybody got up and left the courtroom for the weekend.

Everybody in the courtroom sat down.

Judge Brown said, "The state may call its first witness."

Andy Barrett got back up again and replied, "Thank you, Your Honor. The state calls Bob Andrews to the stand."

The bailiff swore Bob Andrews in.

Andy said, "State your name and occupation for the record."

Bob replied, "Bob Andrews, Cook County coroner."

"How did all the victims die?"

"They were first shot in the head and then stabbed fifteen times before their hair was removed. The victims died before the serial killer stabbed them and cut parts of their hair off."

"Was there anything unusual about their deaths?"

"Yes. The serial killer cut some of their hair off after stabbing his victims fifteen times."

"Why would the serial killer do this?"

"In his sick mind, he wanted a keepsake for his conquest."

"I have no further questions for this witness," Tim replied. "Mister Fields, this is your witness."

Del Fields asked, "Thank you, Your Honor. Could the real serial killer cut off another person's hair in order to frame a person? Yes or no?"

Bob answered, "Yes."

Del said, "I have no further questions for this witness."

Judge Brown said, "You may cross-examine the witness."

Andy asked, "Thank you, Your Honor. Do you think the defendant has a sick mind?"

Bob answered, "To do this crime, the answer is yes."

Andy said, "I have no further questions for this witness."

Judge Brown replied, "You may step down now."

Bob Andrews got up and left the stand. He walked out of the courtroom and returned to his office in the Cook County building.

Andy said, "The state calls Dale Jones to the stand. The bailiff swore Dale Jones in. "State your name and occupation for the record."

Dale replied, "Dale Jones, a police detective for the Arlington Police Department."

Andy asked, "What led you to the defendant, Bill Eck?"

"A 9-1-1 call."

"What did you find with the defendant, Bill Eck?"

"He had a bag with women's hair, a gun, and a knife with blood on it."

"Did you check the fingerprints on the murder weapons?"

"Yes. Both the gun and knife match up with the defendant, Bill Eck."

Andy asked, "Did you check the women's hair and blood on the knife?"

Dale answered, "Yes. They all match the victims."

Judge Tim Brown replied, "The record will show this."

Andy asked, "Have the serial killings stopped in Arlington?"

Dale answered, "Yes."

Andy asked, "How long have you served on the police force?"

Dale answered, "Fifteen years."

Andy said, "Your Honor, I want to declare the police detective, Dale Jones an expert witness."

Judge Brown replied, "The court will do so."

"Thank you, Your Honor," Andy said before turning his attention back to Dale. "In your expert opinion, did you arrest the right person?"

Dale answered, "Yes."

"Do you know if the defendant, Bill Eck, knows how to fire a gun?"

"Yes. Bill has a firearm's identification card. He has firearms at his house and has fired his guns at a gun range according to his family, the Cook County Sheriff Department, and the Springfield Police Department."

Andy said, "I have no further questions for this witness."

Judge Tim Brown replied to Del, "You may question this witness."

Del Fields got up and asked, "How much is the reward for the Arlington Horse Race Track Serial Killer?"

"Fifty thousand dollars."

"Why hasn't anybody come forward to collect this reward money?"

"I don't know."

"Could a person frame my client by making this call to the police and not collect the reward money because he or she would have to come forward? Yes or no?"

"Yes."

"Isn't fifty thousand dollars a lot of money? Yes or no?"

"Yes."

"When did you make Bill Eck your primary suspect? Was it before or after this 9-1-1 call?"

"The 9-1-1 call broke this case wide open for us."

"Is it true that you didn't know who committed this crime until the 9-1-1 call?"

"Yes."

"How long did it take you to get to the scene of the crime to discover my client with all of the evidence?"

"Twenty minutes from the 9-1-1 call."

Del asked, "Is it true that this would be plenty of time to frame my client?"

Dale answered, "Yes."

"If you frame a person, then you would have to stop the killing spree. Is this true?"

"Yes."

Del said, "Your Honor, let the record show that no body claimed the fifty-thousand-dollar reward for the Arlington Horse Race Track Serial Killer. Let the record also show that it took police twenty minutes to get to the scene of the crime. This is plenty of time to call the police up and frame a person with the evidence."

Judge Tim Brown replied, "The record will show this."

Del said, "I have no further questions for this witness."

Del sat back down.

Judge Brown said, "You may cross-examine the witness."

Andy got up. "Thank you, Your Honor. Are you thankful that this person came forward to give you the clues that you needed to solve this case?"

"Yes."

Andy Barrett asked, "In your expert opinion, did somebody frame the defendant, Bill Eck, to cover up the crime?"

Dale answered, "No."

Andy said, "I have no further questions for this witness."

Judge Tim Brown said, "You may step down now."

Dale Jones got up and left the stand. He walked out of the courtroom to his car and returned to the Arlington Police Department.

Andy said, "The state calls Kay Hillson to the stand." The bailiff swore Kay Hillson in.

Andy said, "State your name and occupation for the record."

Kay replied, "Kay Hillson, 9-1-1 dispatcher."

Andy asked, 'Were you on duty when you got the 9-1-1 call about the Arlington Horse Race Track Serial Killer?"

"Yes."

"What did you do?"

"I sent the Arlington police to the location where the serial killer was reported."

"Did you try to get this person's name?"

"Yes."

"What name did he or she give you?"

Kay answered, "A concerned citizen of the community."

"What did he or she want?"

"Justice to be done."

Andy said, "I have no further questions for this witness."

Judge Tim Brown said, "You may question the witness."

Del Fields got up and asked, "What's the reward for catching the Arlington Horse Race Track Serial Killer?"

Kay answered, "Fifty thousand dollars."

"Don't you think it's odd that someone doesn't come forward to collect his or her fifty-thousand-dollar reward?"

"Yes."

Del asked, "Could the real killer claim to be the concerned citizen of the community to want justice to be done while framing my client, Bill Eck, and not come forward in order to protect their identity?"

"Yes."

Del said, "I have no further questions for this witness."

Judge Brown said, "You may cross-examine the witness."

Andy got back up. "Thank you, Your Honor. How often does a person come forward after giving a 9-1-1 call?"

Kay answered, "About half of the time. This is why we have caller identification."

"Where did this call come from?"

"From the payphone at the race track stables."

Andy said, "I have no further questions for this witness."

Judge Tim Brown replied, "You may step down now."

Kay got up from the stand and returned to her seat in the courtroom.

Andy got up and said, "The state calls Tom Jones to the stand."

The bailiff swore Tom Jones in.

Andy said, "State your name and occupation for the record."

Tom replied, "Tom Jones; police detective for the Arlington Police Department."

Andy asked, "How long have you been on the police force?"

He answered, "Ten years."

"Your Honor, I would like to make Detective Tom Jones an expert witness."

Judge Brown replied, "The court will make it so."

Andy asked, "Where was the payphone located?"

"Near the stable entrance."

"Where did you find the defendant?"

"Near the stable entrance."

"What happened to Bill Eck, in your expert opinion?"

"Bill Eck slipped on some horse manure and fell down to cause the bump on his head. He was trying to flee the scene when the accident occurred."

"Were there any shovels or other tools out of place which could have caused the accident?"

"No. We checked this out."

"I have no further questions for this witness."

Judge Tim Brown said, "Your witness."

Del Fields got back up. "Thank you, Your Honor. Do you know for a fact that my client's fall was caused by horse manure in his haste to get out of the stables as fast as he could?"

"No."

"Could a person have called 9-1-1 on this payphone, hit my client over the head, and framed him with the evidence before you arrived at the scene of the crime? Yes or no?"

"Yes."

"I have no further questions for this witness." Del sat back down again.

Judge Brown said, "You may cross-examine this witness."

Andy got up, "Thank you, Your Honor. In your expert opinion, Do you think there's someone framing the defendant, Bill Eck?"

Tom answered "No. We got the right man." Judge Brown said, "You may step down now."

Tom Jones got up from the stand and left the court room. He went outside and got into his car and returned to the police station.

Andy Barrett said, "The state calls Gil Thomas to the stand."

The bailiff swore Gil Thomas in.

Andy replied, "State your name and occupation for the record."

"Gil Thomas; Arlington Police Chief."

"Do you feel good that you have the right person for these serial killings?"

Gil answered, "Yes."

Andy asked, "Is there any pressure on you or your police department to find the Arlington Horse Race Track Serial Killer?"

"No. The public wanted us to stop this crime and find the right person."

"I have no further questions for this witness."

Judge Brown replied, "Your witness."

Del got back up "Thank you, Your Honor. Could a person frame my client, Bill Eck, to cover up his or her crimes?"

"Yes."

Del asked, "Could you lose your job if my client; Bill Eck, is found innocent?"

"Yes."

"Didn't my client, Bill Eck, see you before your detectives arrested him?"

"Yes."

"What was the meeting about?"

"Bill Eck was concerned about my detectives questioning him about talking to Debbie Lewis. He wanted us to stop since he did nothing wrong. He was concerned about people questioning him about what we wanted from him."

Del asked, "Is it true that all my client, Bill Eck, did on this day was to talk to Debbie Lewis? Yes or no?"

Gil answered, "Yes."

"Did my client, Bill Eck, feel that your detectives were harassing him?"

"Yes."

"Did my client, Bill Eck, offer to leave Arlington, the horse race track, and never to come back again?"

"Yes."

"This sounds like an innocent person who just wanted to be left alone."

Andy Barrett got up and replied, "I object to this statement."

Judge Tim Brown responded, "I'll allow it."

Del said, "I have no further questions for this witness." Judge Brown replied, "You may cross-examine the witness."

Andy said, "Thank you, Your Honor. Is anybody framing the defendant?"

Gil answered, "No."

Andy asked, "Is your job safe?"

"Yes."

"In your expert opinion, did the defendant try to get you to call off the dogs?"

"He wanted us off his ass. I wasn't going to do it. This could be our prime suspect, which I was right about."

Andy said, "I have no further questions for this witness."

Judge Tim Brown said, "You may step down now." Gil Thomas got up from the stand and left the courtroom. He talked to reporters as he was leaving for the police station.

Andy said, "The state calls Ray Billows to the stand." The bailiff swore Ray Billows in.

Andy said, "State your name and occupation for the record."

Ray replied, "Ray Billows, Arlington mayor."

Andy asked, "How has Arlington been affected by these crimes?"

Ray answered, "Women are afraid to be alone. People don't feel safe, and are afraid to go to the horse race track in our fine city."

Andy asked, "Are you satisfied with the job your police force is doing?"

Ray answered, "Yes. The city is getting back to nor mal since the arrest of Bill Eck. Women aren't afraid to be alone anymore. All the murders have stopped."

Andy said, "I have no further questions for this witness."

Andy Barrett sat back down again. Judge Tim Brown said, "Your witness."

Del got up. "Thank you, Your Honor. Are you going to run for re-election again?"

"Yes."

Del Fields asked, "Could you get voted out of office if my client, Bill Eck, is found innocent? Yes or no?"

"Yes."

"Could a person be framing my client, Bill Eck, to get away with this crime?"

"Yes."

"Didn't my client, Bill Eck, write a letter to you to get the police off him?"

"Yes."

"Didn't my client, Bill Eck, threaten to move to Arlington to run against you for mayor if you didn't get the police off him?"

"Yes."

Del said, "This sounds like an innocent person who wanted the police to leave him alone. He would go so far as moving to Arlington to run for mayor."

Andy got up and replied, "I object to this statement."

Judge Brown responded, "I'll allow it."

Del said, "I have no further questions for this witness."

Judge Brown said, "You may cross-examine the witness."

Andy responded, "Thank you, Your Honor. Are you going to win the election?"

Ray answered, "Yes."

Andy asked, "Is there anybody framing the defendant?"

"No."

"What did you do with this letter?"

"I gave it to Police Chief Gil Thomas who gave it to his detectives to investigate."

Andy said, "I have no further questions for this witness."

Judge Brown replied, "You may step down now." Ray Billows got up from the stand and left the courtroom. Ray went to the media and told them before he left the courtroom, "Arlington is a safe place now since the Arlington Police Department has arrested this very sick serial killer. Bill Eck is a guilty man and he'll be found guilty as charged soon."

Andy said, "The state calls Joyce Adams to the stand."

The bailiff swore Joyce Adams in.

Andy said, "State your name and occupation for the record."

Joyce replied, "Joyce Adams, secretary."

Andy asked, "What did you see at the horse race track?"

"I saw Bill Eck arguing with both of my friends, Lorrie Franklin and Michele Cook."

"What were they arguing about?"

"Bill winning at the race track."

Andy asked, "Is the person who your friends were arguing with in this courtroom today?"

"Yes. It's the man over there." Joyce pointed to Bill Eck.

Bill was scared to death over this. He knew that he didn't do anything at all, but Joyce was trying to pin the crime on him.

Andy said, "Let the record show that the witness has identified the defendant. I have no further questions for the witness."

Judge Brown said, "Your witness."

Del Fields replied, "Thank you, Your Honor. Aren't you jealous of my client, Bill Eck, by the way that he picks his horses and wins on them?"

Joyce answered, "Yes."

Del asked, "Would you benefit with my client, Bill Eck, out of the way? Yes or no?"

"Yes."

"With my client, Bill Eck, out of the way; you could make a ton of money. Is this true?"

"Yes."

"Do you like Bill Eck?"

"No."

"Could you have framed my client, Bill Eck? Yes or no?"

"No."

Del said, "I have no further questions for this witness."

Judge Brown said, "You may cross-examine this witness."

Andy got up and responded, "Thank you, Your Honor." He then turned his attention to the woman in front of her. "Are you framing the defendant?"

Joyce answered, "No. But nobody likes the defendant since he wins all the time."

Andy said, "I have no further questions for this witness."

Judge Brown replied, "You may step down now."

Joyce Adams got up and left the stand. She then returned to her seat in the courtroom.

Andy said, "The state calls Kim Black to the stand." The bailiff swore Kim Black in. "State your name and occupation for the record."

Kim replied, "Kim Black, receptionist."

Andy asked, "What did you see at the horse race track?"

Kim answered, "I saw my friends, Alice Lang and Maureen Gray, arguing with Bill Eck, who looked at me with evil eyes. This look could have killed somebody."

Andy Barrett asked, "What were they arguing about?"

"Bill Eck winning all of the time."

"Is the defendant capable of killing somebody?" "This evil look makes him capable of killing anybody."

"Is the person who you saw arguing with your friends in the courtroom today?"

"Yes. He's right over there."

Kim pointed right at the fearful Bill Eck, who knew that he never committed any crime.

"Let the record show that the witness has identified the defendant. I have no further questions for this witness."

Andy sat back down again.

Judge Brown said, "Your witness."

Del got back up and spoke, "Thank you, Your Honor. Aren't you jealous, too, of the way that my client, Bill Eck, picks his horses and wins his money?"

"Yes."

"Would you benefit too if my client; Bill Eck, was out of the way? Yes or no?"

Kim answered, "Yes."

"Do you bet on the horses?"

Kim answered, "Yes."

"Is it true that with my client, Bill Eck, out of the way you could cash in at the horse track? Yes or no?"

"Yes."

"Could you be framing my client, Bill Eck, to get back at him for his winnings at the horse track? Yes or no?"

Kim answered, "Yes."

Del said, "I have no further questions for this witness."

Del sat back down again.

Judge Brown said, "You may cross-examine this witness."

Andy got up again. "Thank you, Your Honor. Would you ever frame the defendant for this crime?"

Kim answered, "No."

"I have no further questions for this witness." Judge Brown said, "You may step down now."

Kim Black got up and left the stand. She returned to her seat.

Andy said, "The state calls Steve Gentry to the stand."

The bailiff swore Steve Gentry in.

Andy said, "State your name and occupation for the record."

Steve replied, "Steve Gentry, horse trainer."

"Who do you work for?"

"Roy Simon."

"What's the name of the horse you're training?"

"Cupcake."

Andy asked, "Do you have a problem with the defendant?"

Steve answered, "Yes. He's always getting in the way and telling me how to do my job to make Cupcake a faster horse. Roy Simon has been on him to leave me alone."

Andy said, "I have no further questions for this witness."

Andy sat back down again.

Judge Brown said, "Your witness."

"Thank you, Your Honor," Del said before facing the guy. "Did you want my client, Bill Eck, out of the way?"

Steve answered, "Yes."

"Could you be framing my client, Bill Eck, to get him out of the way? Yes or no?"

"Yes."

Del asked, "Did you get a call from Roy Simon, or somebody pretending to be Roy Simon, at the stables about a meeting for my client, Bill Eck, to go to the stables? Yes or no?"

Steve answered, "Yes."

"What phone was used to call for this meeting?"

"The payphone near the stables."

"After you took Cupcake to the track, where did you go next?"

"I watched the race to cheer on Cupcake to victory."

"Did anybody see you or were you with someone?"

"I was by myself like I always am."

"How long did the race take before you brought Cupcake back to the stables?"

"A half of an hour."

"Did you walk Cupcake to the track by yourself or with somebody else?"

Steve answered, "By myself."

Del asked, "Is it true that you had plenty of time to set up Bill Eck before you brought Cupcake to the race track? Yes or no?"

Steve answered, "Yes."

"I have no further questions for this witness."

Judge Brown replied, "You may cross-examine the witness."

Andy Barrett got up. "Thank you, Your Honor," he said. "Would you frame the defendant to be left alone?"

Steve answered, "No."

"What was the meeting going to be about?"

Steve answered, "Roy Simon wanted to meet Bill Eck to get Bill off of my ass and Larry Synder's ass. Roy was going to let him have it for us and lay the law down to him. Roy just wanted to be the one to do this ass-chewing. I left with Cupcake to the race track after I got the call and gave the message to Bill Eck."

"Do you normally watch the horse races by yourself?"

"Yes. I try to stay out of the way."

"Does Roy Simon use this payphone to get ahold of you or Larry Synder?"

"Yes."

"Does it usually take a half hour for you to bring Cupcake back to the stables after the horse race?"

"Yes."

Del got up and said, "I object. With Bill Eck in prison, then Steve Gentry will get his wish to be left alone."

Andy replied, "I object to this statement."

Judge Brown responded, "Strike this statement from the record. Jurors, make a note of this."

Andy said, "I have no further questions for this witness."

Judge Brown replied, "You may step down now."

Steve Gentry got up and left the stand. He returned to his seat in the courtroom.

Andy said, "The state calls Larry Synder to the stand."

The bailiff swore Larry Synder in.

Andy said, "State your name and occupation for the record."

Larry answered, "Larry Synder, horse jockey."

Without further ado, Andy asked, "Do you work for Roy Simon?"

Larry answered, "Yes."

"What's the name of the horse which you ride?"

"Cupcake."

"Did you have any problems with the defendant?"

"Yes."

"What were the problems?"

"Bill Eck would come to me to tell me how to ride Cupcake to make the horse go faster. This was upsetting me. I didn't need to know how to win a horse race. After all, I have won numerous horse races with Cupcake."

Andy said, "I have no further questions for this witness."

Andy sat back down again.

Judge Brown said, "Your witness."

Del Fields got back up again. "Thank you, Your Honor. Could you be framing my client, Bill Eck, just to be left alone? Yes or no."

Larry answered, "Yes."

Del asked, "Is it true that you wait alone for Cupcake and Steve Gentry to come?"

"Yes."

"How long do you wait?"

"From fifteen minutes to a half an hour."

Del asked, "Do you go to the stables all by yourself?"

"Yes."

"Did you ever use another phone to call the payphone at the stables?"

Larry Synder answered, "Yes."

Del Fields said, "I have no further questions for this witness."

Judge Brown replied, "You may cross-examine this witness."

"Thank you, Your Honor," Andy responded. "Would you be framing the defendant to be left alone?"

Larry answered, "No."

Andy asked, "Is it normal for you to wait alone for Cupcake and Steve Gentry?"

Larry answered, "Yes."

"Why do you use another phone to call the payphone at the stables?"

"To get ahold of Steve Gentry."

"I have no further questions for this witness."

Judge Tim Brown replied, "You may step down now."

Larry Synder got up and left the stand. He returned to his seat.

Andy said, "The state calls Wally Lester to the stand."

The bailiff swore Wally Lester in.

Andy said, "State your name and occupation for the record."

Wally replied, "Wally Lester, outside sales representative."
Andy asked, "Did you file a police report on the defendant?"
Wally answered, "Yes."
"Why?"
"Bill Eck threatened to kill me if I didn't stop arguing with him over his winnings."
"What became of this police report?"
"Nothing. The police saw the police report as a dispute between two parties, not a murder threat."
Andy asked, "Did you see it as a murder threat?"
Wally answered, "Yes. I tried to convince the police otherwise of the report, but the police didn't want to get involved in the dispute."
"Is the defendant capable of killing?"
"Yes."
"I have no further questions for this witness."
Judge Brown said, "Your witness."
"Thank you, Your Honor. Did you file a police report on my client, Bill Eck, to get back at him? Yes or no?" Del Fields asked.
Wally answered, "No."
"Could you be framing my client, Bill Eck?"
"No."
"Do you often lie?"
"No."
"My client never threatened to kill you. Isn't this true?"
"No."
"The police saw my client, Bill Eck, as no threat to you or anybody else. Is this true?"
"No."
"You tried to convince the police that my client, Bill Eck, was a threat. Is this true?"
"No."
"You don't get along with your brother. Isn't this true?"
"No."

Del said, "I have no further questions for this witness."

Judge Brown said, "You may cross-examine the witness."

Andy got up and asked, "Who likes the defendant at the horse racing track?"

Wally answered, "Nobody likes Bill Eck. He upsets everybody because he's always winning all the time."

Andy said, "I have no further questions for this witness."

Judge Brown said, "You may step down now."

Wally Lester got up and left the stand. He returned to his seat.

Andy said, "The state calls Bob Lester to the stand." The bailiff swore Bob Lester in.

Andy Barrett said, "State your name and occupation for the record."

Bob Lester replied, "Bob Lester, sales manager."

Andy asked, "Does Wally Lester work for you?"

Bob answered, "No."

"What did you see on the day that the police report was filed?"

"Bill Eck was winning at the racetrack as usual, but Wally was losing. This was unusual for Wally Lester. Wally went over to Bill Eck and started the argument. I told Wally to leave Bill alone, but he wouldn't listen to me at all. Bill tried to get away from Wally, but Wally wouldn't let him go."

Andy asked, "Do you like Bill Eck?"

Bob answered, "No."

Andy asked, "Why?"

Bob answered, "Bill always wins all of the time."

"I have no further questions for this witness."

"Your witness."

Del Fields got back up again and asked, "Did my client, Bill Eck, ever threaten to kill Wally Lester? Yes or no?"

Bob answered, "No."

"Did the police talk to you about the argument?"

"Yes."

"You don't like your brother, Wally. Isn't this true?"

Bob answered, "Yes."

"Wally lies most of the time to cover up his other lies. Is this true?"

"Yes."

"Could you be framing Bill Eck? Yes or no?"

"Yes."

"I have no further questions for this witness."

Judge Brown said, "You may cross-examine the witness."

Andy got back up again. "Thank you, Your Honor. Would you be framing the defendant?"

Bob answered, "No."

Andy asked, "Is Wally lying at this court trial?"

"No. There were a few mistakes with his testimony."

Andy said, "I have no further questions for this witness."

Judge Brown replied, "You may step down now."

Bob Lester got up and left the stand. He returned to his seat.

Wally Lester, his brother, was upset at Bob Lester for Bob's testimony.

Andy said, "The state calls Karrie Mayo to the stand."

The bailiff swore Karrie Mayo in.

Andy Barrett said, "State your name and occupation for the record."

Karrie Mayo replied, "Karrie Mayo, president of the Chicago Park District."

Andy asked, "Do you get along with the defendant?"

Karrie answered, "I have my concerns about him. I don't trust him."

"What are your concerns?"

Karrie answered, "I don't want him to be around my daughter. He's always arguing with women over his winnings and money."

Andy asked, "Have you seen the defendant argue with any women over winnings and money?"

Karrie answered, "No. But, I have heard of this about this man."

Del got up and said, "I object. This is hearsay."

Judge Brown replied, "The court agrees. Jurors, make a note of this. Hearsay isn't permitted in a court trial. We only deal in facts.

Andy said, "I have no further questions for this witness." Judge Brown said, "Your witness."

"Thank you, Your Honor," Del responded. "Could you be framing my client, Bill Eck, over your concerns?"

Karrie answered, "Yes."

Del Fields asked, "You don't like my client. Isn't this true?"

"Yes."

"Are you the next-door neighbor to the Eeks?"

"Yes."

"Are you worried about the property value going down if my client, Bill Eck, is found guilty? Yes or no?"

Karrie answered, "Yes."

Del said, "I have no further questions for this witness."

Judge Tim Brown said, "You may cross-examine the witness."

Andy replied, "Thank you, Your Honor. Would you be framing the defendant over your concerns or for the property value?"

Karrie answered, "No."

"Does the defendant get along with the rest of the neighbors in the neighborhood?"

Karrie answered, "Yes. He takes care of his own property and goes out for walks in the evening to say 'hi' to the other neighbors when he isn't at the race track."

Del got back up and said, "This sounds like a good neighbor and respectable person of the community. Not a person who you want to lock up."

Andy replied, "I object to this statement."

Judge Brown said, "I'll allow the statement." Del Fields sat back down again.

Andy Barrett said, "I have no further questions for this witness."

Judge Tim Brown replied, "You may step down now."

Karrie Mayo got up and left the stand. She returned to her seat.

Andy said, "The state calls Dave Mayo to the stand." The bailiff swore Dave Mayo in.

Andy said, "State your name and occupation for the record."

Dave replied, "Dave Mayo, accountant."

Andy asked, "Do you like the defendant?"

Dave answered, "No."

"Why don't you like the defendant?"

Dave answered, "He doesn't trust me to do his taxes. He wants to keep his earnings a secret. I do taxes for the neighborhood for a small fee for my services."

Andy asked, "Do you go out to the race track with the defendant?"

Dave answered, "I used to. He keeps on getting into arguments with people over his winnings."

Andy asked, "Did you see him arguing with any of the victims at the horse race track?"

"Yes. All of them."

"Did you hear what they were arguing about?"

"No."

"Is the defendant capable of killing?"

Del Fields got up and said, "I object. The state is leading the witness."

Judge Tim Brown replied, "I'll allow it. Answer the question."

Del sat back down again.

Dave answered, "Yes."

Andy asked, "Are you afraid to have your children near the defendant?"

"Yes."

"I have no further questions for this witness." Andy sat back down again.

Judge Brown said, "Your witness."

"Thank you, Your Honor," Del Fields replied. "Do all of the neighbors do their taxes with you except for my client, Bill Eck?"

"No."

Del asked, "Why are you singling out my client, Bill Eck, in the neighborhood?"

Dave answered, "He did it!"

"How do you know that my client, Bill Eck, did these crimes?"

"I just know it from a gut feeling of mine."

"Are you jealous of my client, Bill Eck, because he wins at the horse race track and you don't? Yes or no?"

Dave answered, "Yes."

"Were you afraid of my client; Bill Eck, before or after his arrest?"

Dave Mayo answered, "After."

Del Fields asked, "Were you afraid for your children's safety before or after my client's arrest?"

"After."

"Is my client, Bill Eck, in your opinion, capable of killing before or after his arrest?

Dave answered, "After."

Del said, "Let the record show that Dave Mayo is afraid of my client, Bill Eck, and for his children's safety after he was arrested. Let the record show that Dave Mayo thinks that my client, Bill Eck, is capable of killing more people after his arrest."

Judge Tim Brown replied, "The record will show this."

Del said, "I have no further questions for this witness."

Del sat back down again.

Judge Brown responded, "You may cross-examine the witness."

"Thank you, Your Honor," Andy replied. "Would you be framing the defendant?"

Dave answered, "No."

"I have no further questions for this witness."

Judge Brown said, "You may step down now."

Dave Mayo got up and left the stand. He returned to his seat to be next to his wife, Karrie.

Andy Barrett said, "The state calls Roy Simon to the stand."

Roy Simon replied, "Roy Simon, owner of Roy Simon Engineers."

"Did you hear about all of the complaints from the horse race track about the defendant?"

"Yes."

"What did you do about all of these complaints?"

Roy answered, "I sat down with Bill Eck and talked to him about all of these complaints at the horse race track."

"Do you own a horse?"

"Yes."

"What's the name of the horse?"

"Cupcake."

"Did you fire the defendant?"

"Yes."

"Why did you fire the defendant?"

Roy answered, "Nobody wanted to work with a serial killer or believed that Bill Eck was innocent. They were all afraid of him, especially the women. People didn't want to do business with us unless we got rid of Bill Eck."

Andy asked, "Did the defendant go to the horse race track on the weekends?"

Roy answered, "Yes."

"I have no further questions for this witness." Andy sat back down again.

Judge Brown said, "Your witness."

Del Fields got back up again and asked, "Thank you, Your Honor. Did all of the complaints happen to my client, Bill Eck, from the women before or after my client was arrested?"

Roy answered, "After."

Del asked, "My client, Bill Eck, was a good employee up until he was arrested. Is this true? Yes or no?"

Roy answered, "Yes."

"Could you be framing your own employee?"

"Yes."

Del said, "I have no further questions for this witness."

Del sat back down again.

Judge Brown said, "You may cross-examine this witness."

Andy got back up. "Thank you, Your Honor. Would you frame the defendant?"

Roy answered, "No. I would lose business if I did this. He has never done anything to my business yet except for being arrested for this crime and this trial."

Andy said, "I have no further questions for this witness."

Judge Brown replied, "You may step down now."

Roy Simon got up and left the stand. He left the courtroom and returned to his office to run his business.

Andy Barrett said, "The state calls Jill Simon to the stand."

The bailiff swore Jill Simon in.

Andy said, "State your name and occupation for the record."

Jill Simon replied, "Jill Simon, secretary."

Andy asked, "Are you afraid of the defendant?"

Jill answered, "Yes."

"Why are you afraid of the defendant?"

"Because he did this crime."

Del got up and said, "I object. The witness is just stating this, and it hasn't been proven."

Andy replied, "I withdraw the question. I have no further questions for this witness."

Andy sat back down again.

Judge Brown said, "Your witness."

Del Fields replied, "Thank you, Your Honor. Did you like your employee, Bill Eck, before or after he got arrested?"

Jill answered, "Before."

Del asked, "Could you be framing your employee Bill Eck? Yes or no?"

Jill answered, "Yes."

Del said, "I have no further questions for this witness."

Del sat back down again.

Judge Brown said, "You may cross-examine the witness."

Andy got back up. "Thank you, Your Honor," he said. "Would you be framing the defendant?"

Jill answered, "No. We have our business to lose if we did something like that."

Andy Barrett said, "I have no further questions for this witness."

Judge Brown said, "You may step down now."

Jill Simon got up and left the stand. She left the courtroom to return to her office to help Roy run their business.

Andy said, "The state rests."

Judge Brown said, "We'll hear the defense case tomorrow."

The bailiff replied, "All rise."

Everybody got up. Judge Brown got up and left the courtroom. Then everybody else left the courtroom.

The guards came in and placed handcuffs on Bill Eck.

They took Eck back to jail.

6

DEFENSE

The bailiff said, "All rise. The Honorable Tim Brown presiding."

Everybody stood up.

Judge Tim Brown walked into the courtroom and took his seat.

Everybody sat back down again.

Judge Brown said, "The defense may call its first witness."

Del Fields replied, "Thank you, Your Honor. The defense calls Ed Michaels to the stand."

The bailiff swore Ed Michaels in.

Del Fields asked, "Are you best friends with the defendant?"

Ed answered, "Yes."

"Are you still best friends with the defendant since his arrest?"

"Yes."

"Are you afraid of the defendant?"

"No."

"Do you believe the defendant could commit these crimes?"

"No."

"Do you still work for Roy Simon Engineers?"

"Yes."

Del said, "I have no further questions for this witness," and sat back down again.

Judge Brown said, "Your witness."

Andy Barrett got back up again. "Thank you, Your Honor. Were you a witness to a court order of Mary Eck?"

Ed Michaels answered, "Yes."

"In this court order, did the defendant hit his wife? Yes or no?"

"Yes."

"Does the defendant have a bad temper?"

"Yes."

"Were you ever afraid that the defendant would kill his wife?"

"Yes."

Andy said, "I have no further questions for this witness."

Andy sat back down again.

Judge Brown said, "You may cross-examine the witness."

Del replied, "Thank you, Your Honor. Did the defendant serve any time on this court order filed by Mary Eck?"

Ed answered, "No. Mary dropped the court order."

"Where did the defendant stay during this court order?"

Ed answered, "With me."

"Were you afraid of the defendant then?"

"No."

"Are you afraid of the defendant now?"

"No."

Del Fields said, "I have no further questions for this witness."

Judge Brown replied, "You may step down now."

Ed Michaels got up and left the stand. He returned to his seat in the courtroom.

Del said, "The defense calls Father Franks to the stand."

The bailiff swore Father Franks in.

Del asked, "Are you the pastor of the defendant?"

Father Franks answered, "Yes."

Del asked, "Are you afraid of the defendant?"

Father Franks answered, "No."

"Is there anyone in your parish afraid of the defendant?"

"No."

"What's the parish doing for the defendant?"

Father Franks answered, "We're raising money for his legal defense fund to prove him innocent of these charges."

"Did you counsel both Bill and Mary Eck after the fight that separated this couple?"

"Yes. Their love for one another brought this couple back together again. Bill Eck gave his word that he would never hurt Mary again. Bill has never done this again."

Del said, "I have no further questions for this witness."

Del sat back down again.

Judge Tim Brown said, "Your witness."

Andy replied, "Thank you, Your Honor. Are you sure that the defendant kept his word to his wife about not hitting her again?"

Father Franks answered, "No, I'm not."

"I have no further questions for this witness." Andy sat back down again.

Judge Brown said, "You may cross-examine this witness."

"Thank you, Your Honor. Have you done any more counseling sessions for Bill and Mary Eck since the fight?"

"No."

Del said, "I have no further questions for this witness."

Judge Brown said, "You may step down now."

Father Franks got up and left the stand. He walked out of the courtroom and returned to his parish to do his duties for the Lord.

Del said, "The defense calls Eddie Eck to the stand." The bailiff swore Eddie Eck in.

He then asked, "Do you believe in your brother's innocence?"

Eddie answered, "Yes."

"Have you set up a legal defense fund for your brother?"

"Yes."

"Have you given your own money from your own gas station for your brother's legal defense fund?"

Eddie Eck answered, "Yes."

"I have no further questions for this witness." Del sat back down again.

Judge Brown said, "Your witness."

"Thank you, Your Honor. Were you a witness to a court order filed by Mary Eck over a fight between Bill and Mary Eck?"

Eddie answered, "Yes."

Andy said, "I have no further questions for this witness."

Judge Brown said, "You may cross-examine the witness."

Del got back up. "Thank you, Your Honor. Did you actually witness the fight between Bill and Mary Eck?"

Eddie answered "No."

"Has the defendant ever threatened to kill you?" Eddie answered, "Yes. He said it while he was upset."

Del asked, "Has the defendant ever meant to kill you?"

Eddie answered, "No." He said this while he was upset.

Del said, "I have no further questions for this witness."

Judge Tim Brown said, "You may step down now."

Eddie Eck got up and left the stand. He returned to his seat in the courtroom.

Del said, "The defense calls Mary Eck to the stand." The bailiff swore Mary Eck in.

Del Fields asked, "Are you frightened of your husband?"

Mary Eck answered, "No."

"Has your husband ever threatened to kill you?" Mary answered, "Yes."

"Did your husband mean this threat?"

"No. This is the reason why I dropped the court order."

"I have no further questions for this witness." Del sat back down again.

Judge Brown said, "Your witness."

"Thank you, Your Honor. Did you lie to the court about the court order filed or to this court?"

Mary answered, "No."

Andy said, "I have no further questions for this witness."

Judge Brown said, "You may cross-examine this witness."

Del replied, "I don't wish to cross-examine the witness."

Judge Brown said, "You may step down now."

Mary Eck got up and left the stand. She returned to her seat next to Eddie Eck in the courtroom.

Del Fields said, "The defense calls Charlie Eck to the stand."

The bailiff swore Charlie Eck in.

Del asked, "Are you afraid of your father?"

Charlie answered, "No."

"I have no further questions for this witness." Del sat back down again.

Judge Brown said, "Your witness."

"Thank you, Your Honor. Were you a witness of a court order filed by Mary Eck over a fight between Bill and Mary Eck?"

Charlie answered, "Yes."

Andy asked, "In this court order, did Bill Eck threaten to kill Mary Eck? Yes or no?"

"Yes."

"I have no further questions for this witness." Andy sat back down again.

Judge Brown said, "You may cross-examine the witness."

"Thank you, Your Honor. Did you actually see your father threaten to kill your mother or did you hear the argument?"

Charlie answered, "I heard it."

Del Fields said, "I have no further questions for this witness."

Judge Tim Brown replied, "You may step down now."

Charlie Eck got up and left the stand. He returned to his seat in the courtroom next to his mother.

Del said, "The defense calls Bob Eck to the stand." The bailiff swore Bob Eck in.

Del then asked, "Are you afraid of your father?"

Bob answered, "No."

Del said, "I have no further questions for this witness."

Andy replied, "I have no questions for this witness." Judge Tim Brown said, "You may step down now."

Bob Eck got up and left the stand. He returned to his seat next to his brother in the courtroom.

Del said, "The defense calls Carrie Eck to the stand." The bailiff swore Carrie Eck in.

Del asked, "Are you afraid of your father?" Carrie answered, "No."

"I have no further questions for this witness."

Andy replied, "I have no questions for this witness."

Judge Brown said, "You may step down now."

Carrie Eck got up and left the stand. She returned to her seat next to her brother in the courtroom.

Del Fields said, "The defense rests."

Judge Tim Brown replied, "We'll hear closing arguments tomorrow."

The bailiff replied, "All rise."

Judge Brown got up and left the courtroom. Everybody got up and left the courtroom.

The guards placed handcuffs on Bill Eck and took him back to the Cook County jail.

7

CLOSING

The bailiff said, "All rise."

Everybody got up from their seat.

Judge Tim Brown walked in and sat down. Everybody sat down in the courtroom.

Judge Brown said, "The state will give its closing argument first."

Andy Barrett got up and replied, "Thank you, Your Honor. Ladies and gentlemen of the jury. The defendant was found with the murder weapons and the hair of his victims. The defense has never proven their case. The defendant is the Arlington Horse Race Track Serial Killer. He's not being framed for these crimes at all. The state has proven its case. The police did their jobs. Now it's time that you do your job and convict the defendant on all of the charges against him. This is an open-and-shut case."

Andy sat back down again.

Judge Brown said, "It's the defense's turn now."

Del Fields got up and replied, "Thank you, Your Honor. Ladies and gentlemen of the jury. This isn't an open-and-shut case like the state wants you to believe. The real serial killer framed my client, Bill Eck. The real serial killer is out on the loose to kill more people. My client, Bill Eck, is a hard-working individual who did a good job until he was arrested on these false charges. His only crime is that he had a passion on the weekends to go to the horse track to bet on the horses.

My client, Bill Eck, tried to give advice to his boss's horse jockey and trainer, who didn't like it at all. My client, Bill Eck, is innocent of all charges. Send this case back to the authorities, so they can do their jobs to find the real serial killer."

Del Fields sat back down.

8

VERDICT

Judge Tim Brown said to the jury, "Take as much time as you need to come up with the right decision in this case. Weigh all of the evidence and testimony to determine whether the defendant, Bill Eck, is the Arlington Horse Track Serial Killer or not."

The jury left the room to decide the fate of Bill Eck. After a week of debating over the case, the jury came back.

Judge Brown asked, "Has the jury come up with a verdict?"

The foreman of the jury answered, "Yes, we have, Your Honor."

Judge Brown said, "Please read the verdict to the court."

Both Del Fields and Bill Eck were standing now.

The foreman of the jury said, "We, the jury, find the defendant, Bill Eck, in the matter of the State of Illinois versus Bill Eck, guilty as charged on all counts."

Bill Eck was saddened and shocked by the verdict. He couldn't figure out how the jury could find him guilty as charged on all counts.

Del Fields didn't know what happened either. He thought that he should have won the case, not lost it.

Judge Brown said, "I give the defendant, Bill Eck, life imprisonment without parole for these brutal crimes."

Del now turned to the frightened Bill Eck and said, "We'll appeal this decision. We'll get you out of prison."

Bill replied, "I hope so."

The guards came in and placed handcuffs on Bill Eck. They took him to the Cook County jail waiting for his trip to prison.

Andy Barrett shook hands with the victims' families. He knew that he had his man and the right man was go ing to prison. Then he left the courtroom to talk to the me dia about the successful case.

The top story in Chicago was the verdict at Cook County courthouse of Bill Eck being found guilty of all charges.

A week later, Bill Eck was transferred to the prison in Pontiac, Illinois, to serve his lifelong sentence.

9

PRISON

Bill Eck met Tim Monroe, Carl Hinds, and Don Ever more.

Tim Monroe was in prison for murdering his neighbors who tried to shortchange him on a sale. He liked do ing everything his way. He was in prison for life for his crimes.

Carl Hinds was in prison for murdering his friends over questioning him over his version of the Bible. He believed in God if it suited his purpose. He believed that everybody would go to Hell if they wouldn't believe in God like he did. He knew his Bible and used it to serve his purpose. He was in prison for life for his crimes.

Don Evermore was in prison for murdering his family. He always claimed that he was innocent of all charges, but nobody wanted to listen to him after his conviction. He had a court-appointed attorney who was fresh out of college. He blamed the court-appointed attorney for him being in prison. He was in prison for life for his crimes, too.

On the first day of being in prison, Tim Monroe said to Bill Eck, "This is my bunk."

Bill Eck replied, "Then I'll take the top bunk."

Bill just wanted to be reasonable and make do of his stay in prison.

Tim Monroe responded, "This is my bunk too."

Tim Monroe was looking for a fight. He wanted to show Bill Eck who was the boss of this prison and this cell.

Bill Eck was confused now and asked, "Where do I sleep?"

Tim Monroe answered, "The floor."

Bill Eck wasn't going to give in to Tim Monroe now and said, "I'm not sleeping on the floor, but in one of these bunks."

Tim Monroe hit Bill Eck with his right hand in a punch from the back as hard as he could. Bill went for ward and hit the bunks with his head. Bill was knocked out cold. Tim, meanwhile, proceeded to beat the living tar out of Bill until the guards got there to save Bill's life.

Bill was taken to the hospital for the beating that he took from Tim Monroe.

After finding out about the beating, Del Fields went to Steve Owens, the warden, and said, "I don't like this beating of my client from his roommate. Why can't you protect your prisoners, especially from themselves?"

Steve answered, "I run the prison. It's a strict prison. We're seeking more charges against Tim Monroe for beat ing up your client."

Del said, "I want you to do something to protect my client here while I get him an appeal on these false charges against him. He's an innocent man."

Steve replied, "I have heard this story before over and over again. They're all alike. They're all guilty as charged."

Del responded, "Well, I'm going to prove to you and the world that my client is an innocent man."

Steve replied, "I'll get him a different roommate. Will this satisfy you?"

Del answered, "Yes, for now."

Del Fields left the warden's office.

After Bill Eck recovered from his injuries and was released from the hospital, Steve Owens, the warden, was true to his word and sent the fully recovered Bill Eck to Don Evermore's cell.

A week later, Don Evermore said, "I'm an innocent man. Somebody is framing me for the deaths of my family. I wish that I knew who the sons-of-bitches were because I would kill them for having me suffer like this."

Bill Eck replied, "I'm an innocent man too. Somebody is framing me over the deaths of five women at the Arlington Horse Track."

The guards turned out the lights and they went to sleep.

A month later, Mary Eck came to visit her husband and said, "Hi, Bill. How are you doing?"

Bill answered, "I got beat up by my first roommate. I'm in prison for a crime that I didn't commit. I'm doing the best that I can do under the circumstances."

Mary said, "Eddie believes in you. He lost his gas station. Now, he's working for somebody else. They're going to make a funeral home at the site of his old gas station. We had to move out of our house to an apartment because the neighbors didn't want us there. We couldn't afford our house anymore. I got a job to support the family. Charlie left the minor league baseball team to get a job. He has moved in with me in the apartment.

"We sold all of the furniture. We put this money into the bank to pay our bills. Bob Eck is still in the minor leagues. He gives us money that he can afford to live without to support us. We're doing everything that we can do to get you out of here. We know that you're an innocent man.

Bill Eck said, "Thank you for the news and the sup port from home. I wish that I could be there for you."

Mary Eck replied, "I want you out of here too."

Bill responded, "I don't know how long that I'll be in here before they file an appeal. I want you to find yourself another man to take care of you."

Mary said, "I don't want to love another man. I love you for who you are. I'll wait a lifetime to get you out of here."

Bill replied, "I love you too."

Mary said, "I wish that I could kiss you now, but I can't. I hate this place and this wall which separates us from each other."

She left crying again. She hated to go to this place and see her husband suffer like this.

Six months later, Carl Hinds started a Bible study class. He taught the Bible the way that he believed in the Lord.

Bill Eck went to Carl's Bible study group to get to the Lord. He didn't agree with the teachings of Carl or believe in the God that Carl believed in. He left after giving the Bible study group a try.

Carl Hinds asked, "Why don't you want to attend my Bible study group?"

Bill Eck answered, "You know your Bible but you don't know God or believe in God."

Carl said, "Yes, I do and you will attend the next session."

Bill just walked away from Carl, who followed him. Carl punched Bill in the back of the head. They both got into a fight over how a Bible study group was supposed to be taught.

Minutes later, the guards broke the fight up and took them to see Steve Owens, the warden.

Owens said, "Bill Eck and Carl Hinds, just because you disagree with the teaching of a Bible study group, you don't get into a fight over it. Do I make myself clear?"

Both Bill and Carl answered, "Yes, Sir."

A year later, Father Franks came to visit Bill Eck and said, "We've all been praying for you."

Bill Eck replied, "I'm praying to God to lift this cross away from me."

Father Franks responded, "God will get rid of this suffering for you in His Own Time."

Bill said, "I wish that it was sooner."

Father Franks replied, "You can't speed up the Lord's Time. His Time is the best time for everybody. You'll see someday."

Father Franks gave Bill Eck a blessing and then left to go back to his church.

10

APPEAL

Six months later, Del Fields examined the trial record for an appeal.

Del Fields went to Judge Tim Brown and said, "The police had no suspect for this crime until the 9-1-1 call was given to them. We would like a new trial to really cross-examine these detectives."

Judge Tim Brown turned to one witness, Arlington Police Chief Gil Thomas, and asked, "Police Chief Gil Thomas, will this change the testimony of the Arlington Police Department?"

Gil Thomas answered, "No."

Andy Barrett asked, "In your expert opinion, is Bill Eck, a good or bad citizen of the community?"

Gil answered, "Bad citizen of the community."

Andy said, "This is one man's opinion against another man's opinion. The defense is on a wild goose chase for an appeal to get their client out of prison."

Judge Brown said, "I agree with the state. Do you have any other items to be cross-examined for an appeal?"

Del answered, "No. Not at this time, Your Honor."

A day later, Del said to Mary Eck, "We lost our appeal, but are still looking for holes in the case for another shot at an appeal."

Mary Eck replied, "I'm praying that we can find an answer to get my husband out of prison."

11

MEDIA

A year later, Del Fields said to Mary Eck, "Mary, we're going to the media, the talk shows, and television to put the pressure on the State of Illinois to release your husband."

Mary Eck answered, "That sounds good."

Del said, "I hope that you're ready to talk to the media, the talk shows, and television about Bill and why you believe that he's innocent."

Mary answered, "I am."

A month later, Del Fields and Mary Eck went to the prison to see Bill. They told the impressed Bill Eck their plan about getting his story to the media, the talk shows, and the television viewers.

Bill said to Del and Mary, "I have heard of this before. First, it was an appeal that didn't work out at all. Now, it's this plan. I'll believe this plan when I see it."

Mary replied, "Honey, we're doing everything that we can to get you out of this awful prison. You don't belong here, since you never committed these crimes."

Bill responded, "I know that you're doing what you can to get me out of prison."

Both Del Fields and Mary Eck left the prison to get Bill out of prison by starting their plan.

A month later, Mary told of the hardships her family was going through since the conviction of her husband, to the media, the talk shows, and to the television viewers. Mary Eck said, "Bill is an innocent man. The real killer will strike sometime soon. The police never knew who the real killer was. A 9-1-1 call and the planting of murder evidence led the police to my husband, who has always maintained his innocence. The State of Illinois was looking for a conviction and got one. This crime isn't solved at all. We need to place pressure on the State of Illinois to drop these charges against my husband and solve this terrible crime. My husband has no criminal record and was treated like a criminal. My husband would never harm a person, especially a woman."

A week later, Andy Barrett and Gil Thomas gave a press conference.

Andy said, "We, the State of Illinois, have our man. It was Bill Eck who committed these crimes. Bill Eck is the Arlington Horse Track Serial Killer. All of the serial killings have stopped since Bill Eck was arrested and convicted of these crimes. We feel sorry for all of the hardships of the Eck family, but their hardships will not get Bill Eck out of prison."

Mary Eck was saddened by the news. She hoped that the State of Illinois would drop these charges, but they refused to. Now, she didn't know what to do.

Del Fields knew that he had to do something to get Bill Eck out of prison, but he didn't know what to do. So far, the State of Illinois was winning every round.

12

MURDERS

A year later in Chicago at Navy Pier, the Chicago Police found Phyllis Brown, who was shot in the head and stabbed fifteen times. The police were clueless as to who committed this crime.

A month later near Lake Michigan in Chicago, the Chicago Police found Gaye Mills. She was killed the same way that Phyllis Brown was.

Tom Plant, a Chicago Police detective, knew about the case of Bill Eck versus the People of Illinois. He went to the library and the Cook County Courthouse to research the old case. He found out that the other five victims died the same way that the two victims in Chicago had.

A week later, Tom Plant called Gil Thomas on the phone and said, "Either you have arrested the wrong per son for the crime at the horse track years ago or we have a copycat killer. I think that you have arrested the wrong man and convicted the wrong man. I have two victims in Chicago who have been killed the same way that the other five victims were."

Gil replied, "Mary Eck and Del Fields have been stirring things up. They have probably shown people how Bill Eck killed his victims."

Tom responded, "Well, I don't think so. I'm going to visit Bill Eck in prison to listen to his side of the story and to learn how he killed his victims."

Tom Plant hung up the phone.

He went to Pontiac to the prison to see Bill Eck. Tom stated, "I'm Detective Tom Plant with the Chicago Police Department. Why did you kill these victims?"

Bill answered, "I don't know what you're talking about because I never killed a soul."

Tom asked, "Why did you shoot your victims?"

Bill answered, "I told you that I didn't do these crimes."

"Why did you stab your victims fifteen times?"

"I told you that I didn't do these crimes. How many times do I have to tell you this?"

Tom asked, "If you didn't do these crimes, then who did?"

Bill answered, "The person who killed these women planted the criminal evidence on me at the stables and set up a meeting for me to go to."

Tom asked, "Did you tell the Arlington Police of your innocence?"

Bill answered, "Yes. They weren't interested in the truth. They were only interested in an arrest and getting a conviction."

Tom now realized the miscarriage of justice and said, "I'll work with your attorney, Del Fields, to get you out of here. Hopefully, we can get you out of here soon. You have suffered far too long in here."

Tom left the prison and returned to Chicago.

A day later, Tom called Gil up again and said, "I have talked to Bill Eck. He's an innocent man. I would like to find the person who is framing him."

Gil Thomas replied, "I'm sure that Bill gave you an act. He tried to be an actor at his trial and to us, but we didn't believe this act."

Tom said, "I'm sure that this is no act. Bill Eck is an innocent man. I'm going to try to get him out of prison soon."

Gil Thomas replied, "Good luck." The phone conversation ended.

A week later, Tom went to see Del and said, "I have talked to your client about this crime. I'm positive that he's an innocent man."

Del replied, "I have been working on getting people to talk to the government about getting my client out of prison. So far, nothing has worked out."

Tom responded, "I'll give you a hand with this case. This case will also help me out with my case. I would like to catch the person who framed Bill Eck and committed these seven murders."

Del said, "This sounds good." Tom then left Del's office.

13

RELEASE

In Chicago at the Chicago Police Department, Detective Tom Plant called for a press conference. Del Fields was in the background.

Tom said, "The Chicago Police Department is searching for the killer or the killers of the Arlington Horse Track Serial Killer. We don't agree with the City of Arlington that Bill Eck did these crimes. We believe that somebody else framed Bill Eck to cover up these five kill ings in Arlington and has struck again in our city with two more serial killings."

The media and the people of Arlington were placing pressure on the State of Illinois to drop the charges against Bill Eck now. They believed the Chicago Police Detective Tom Plant.

Andy Barrett didn't know what to do now. He said to himself, "Am I going to cave in to the pressure of the people and the media now? Is my case rock solid? Is Bill Eck an innocent man? Did I convict an innocent man?"

Andy had no answers to these questions.

Mary Eck just prayed to God that Bill would be coming home soon since these serial killings in Chicago proved their case that Bill was an innocent man.

A week later, Del was called into the office of the state's attorney.

Andy said, "We believe that we have the right person but the media and the people are on us about whether Bill Eck is innocent or guilty. These murders in Chicago have got all of us confused. We believe that you started all of this up and created a copycat killer, but the media and the people are on our asses. We'll release Bill Eck to you on your own recognizance. If he commits one crime, he'll be back into prison so fast that you couldn't blink an eyelid. Make this clear to Bill."

Del Fields said, "We'll take the deal. We'll show you that Bill Eck is an innocent man."

A day later, Del traveled to the prison in Pontiac. Del told the shocked Bill Eck about his freedom and the conditions of his freedom.

Bill Eck replied, "I'll be good. I don't plan to commit any crimes, but want to make up for the lost time to my wife and family. They have been waiting for me to get out of prison. It'll be different to be out of here and to be with my family."

Mary Eck was glad to have her husband back. She only wished that the police would catch the real killer and all the charges could be dropped.

14

KILLER

Mary wanted to keep Bill safe. She was afraid that the killer might come after her husband. She didn't want any more problems that could send her husband back into prison again.

A week later in Arlington, the police found Bob Lester. He was shot three times in the head. The police had no clues as to what happened to him.

Bill Eck was at church when the killing took place. Bill refused to go to Arlington since he had very bad memories there.

Dale and Tom Jones immediately came to visit Bill Eck. Dale asked, "Where were you?"

Bill answered, "At church with my wife."

Dale asked, "Did you have anything against Bob Lester?"

Bill answered, "No."

Dale said, "We'll be in touch."

The media and the people wanted to know if Bob Lester's murder had anything to do with the serial kill ings years ago. The Arlington Police had no answers to these questions except that it was under investigation.

Bill Eck was upset at the fact that the Arlington Police were questioning him about Bob Lester's murder. He knew that the Arlington Police were trying to pin all of these crimes on him.

A week later, Bill Eck went to the store to pick up some groceries.

While he was gone, the killer came to the Eeks' house and took Mary and Carrie Eck hostage. He planned to kill both of them because he wanted to get even with Bill Eck for getting out of prison.

Fifteen minutes later, Bill came back from the store.

He called, "I'm back!"

There was no answer and this was odd.

Bill opened the door to the living room and saw Wally Lester holding his wife and daughter hostage.

Wally said, "I don't like women. I have the power now. Look what I can do."

Bill rushed over to Wally without thinking of safety for himself.

Wally was shocked and fired his gun at Bill, but it missed.

Bill grabbed the gun and both Bill and Wally fought over it. The gun went off three times. All three bullets hit Wally in the chest.

While Wally lay dying, he said, "I lied at the court trial to get to you. I hated you for winning at the horse race track all the time. I always told you that I would get you back someday. I don't like my brother at all. No one will ever take me alive."

Then Wally Lester died.

Both Mary and Carrie hugged Bill while they were crying. They were so relieved that the killer could never bother them again.

IS
END

The State of Illinois dropped all the charges against Bill Eck after the Illinois State Police collected all the evidence in the case. The State Police ruled that Wally Lester was the Arlington Horse Race Track Serial Killer and Bill Eck had been falsely convicted of the crime.

The Eck family moved from Chicago to Chatham. Bill Eck sued the State of Illinois and the City of Arlington for ten million dollars and won.

Bill Eck sued Roy Simon Engineers for five million dollars for falsely firing him and won this case too.

Afterward, he went to work for a local engineering company in Springfield.

Bob Eck made it to the Major Leagues with the Chicago Cubs. He'll never forget how the Arlington Police Department arrested his father on these false charges.

Roy Billows lost his re-election bid for the City of Arlington.

Gil Thomas left the Arlington Police Department due to pressure from the public. He went to a small town in Wisconsin to be the police chief there.

Bill Eck has never forgotten about his experience with the law and how he was falsely convicted of a crime he didn't commit. Bill Eck was guilty of nothing.

CPSIA information can be obtained
at www.ICGtesting.com
Printed in the USA
BVHW060050180223
658747BV00018B/1557